April & Mae
and the
Sleepover

EVERY DAY
WITH
April & Mae

SUNDAY

MONDAY

TUESDAY

WEDNESDAY

THURSDAY

FRIDAY

SATURDAY

Collect them ALL!

April & Mae

and the

Sleepover

THE FRIDAY BOOK

MEGAN DOWD LAMBERT

Illustrated by GISELA BOHÓRQUEZ

ini Charlesbridge

To my daughter Natayja, who is a night owl and
a good friend. I love you and am so lucky to be
your mom.—M. D. L.

To my mom, the person I love the most in the world.
—G. B.

Published by Charlesbridge
9 Galen Street, Watertown, MA 02472 • (617) 926-0329 • www.charlesbridge.com

Library of Congress Cataloging-in-Publication Data
Names: Lambert, Megan Dowd, author. | Bohórquez, Gisela, illustrator.
Title: April & Mae and the sleepover: the Friday book / Megan Dowd Lambert;
    illustrated by Gisela Bohórquez.
Other titles: April and Mae and the sleepover
Description: Watertown, MA: Charlesbridge, [2023] | Series: Every day with
    April & Mae | Audience: Ages 5–8 | Summary: "April and Mae are best friends
    (and so are their pets). When April plans a backyard sleepover, Mae isn't sure
    about sleeping in the tent. Together they make the space more comfortable
    and fall asleep to scary stories."—Provided by publisher.
Identifiers: LCCN 2021029013 (print) | LCCN 2021029014 (ebook) |
    ISBN 9781623542634 (hardcover) | ISBN 9781632898562 (ebook)
Subjects: LCSH: Best friends—Juvenile fiction. | Friendship—Juvenile fiction.
    | Sleepovers—Juvenile fiction. | Backyard camping—Juvenile fiction. |
    CYAC: Best friends—Fiction. | Friendship—Fiction. | Sleepovers—Fiction. |
    Camping—Fiction.
Classification: LCC PZ7.1.L26 Am 2023 (print) | LCC PZ7.1.L26 (ebook) |
    DDC 813.6 [E]—dc23
LC record available at https://lccn.loc.gov/2021029013

Printed in China
(hc) 10 9 8 7 6 5 4 3 2 1

The art herein is drawn in the style of the series characters originally
    illustrated by Briana Dengoue.
Illustrations done in Photoshop
Display type set in Jacoby by Adobe
Text type set in Grenadine by Markanna Studios Inc.
Printed by 1010 Printing International Limited in Huizhou, Guangdong, China
Production supervision by Jennifer Most Delaney
Designed by Cathleen Schaad

April and Mae plan
the best sleepovers.

Sometimes April and her dog
go to Mae's house.
Sometimes Mae and her cat
go to April's house.

Mae is a night owl.
April is not.
April is an early bird.
Mae is not.
But April and Mae are friends.
Best friends.
And their pets
are best friends, too.

One Friday, April and Mae
have a sleepover at April's house.
"I have a fun plan," says April.
"What is it?" asks Mae.
"We will camp out in my backyard!"
says April.
"We will?" asks Mae.

"We will sleep in sleeping bags
   under the stars," says April.
"That sounds chilly," says Mae.
"We will be in a tent," says April.
"OK," says Mae.

"What is the fun part?"asks Mae.
"We will sing songs
   and tell scary stories," says April.

"OK," says Mae.

"We will make s'mores,"
 says April.
"OK," says Mae.

"Does that sound fun?" asks April.
"Sleeping bags, stars, songs, s'mores,
and scary stories are fun," says Mae.

"Yes!" says April.

"But I like to be comfy," says Mae.

"Camping can be comfy," says April.

Mae is not sure about that.

April and Mae go to April's backyard.
"We need a flat spot
for the tent," says April.
April's dog sniffs the ground.
Mae's cat paws the grass.
"Woof!" says April's dog.
"Meow!" says Mae's cat.
"It is *almost* flat," says April.
"Almost," says Mae.

April and Mae pitch the tent.
There are many steps to follow.
There are strings
and stakes
and poles.
It takes a long time.

"TA-DA!" says April at last.
April and Mae go inside the tent.
April's dog and Mae's cat
go inside, too.

They lie down
in their sleeping bags.

"Ahhh," says April.

"Ugh!" says Mae.

"What is wrong?" asks April.
"The ground is hard," says Mae.

April gets pillows
from her house.
"Pillows!" says April.

"Thank you," says Mae.
"You are welcome," says April.

"Woof?" says
April's dog.

"Meow?" says
Mae's cat.

"They need pillows, too," says Mae.

April gets pillows for the pets.
Everyone is comfy now.

It is getting dark.

"We can look at the stars," says April.

"But I am so comfy now," says Mae.

"We can look at the stars
from inside the tent," says April.

"How?" asks Mae.

"I will unzip the windows," says April.

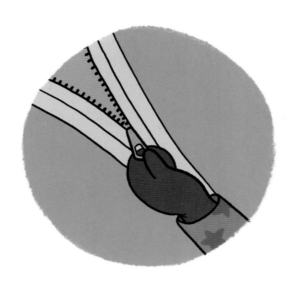

April gets up.
There are many zippers
and ties and flaps.

25

April lies down.
April and Mae look at the stars.
A shooting star sails by.
"Make a wish!" says April.

"I wish for a blanket," says Mae.
"Are you chilly?" asks April.
"There is a breeze now," says Mae.
April gets a blanket for Mae.

"Thank you," says Mae.

"You're welcome," says April.

April lies down again.

Mae's cat curls up on top of Mae.

April yawns a big yawn.

April's dog yawns, too.

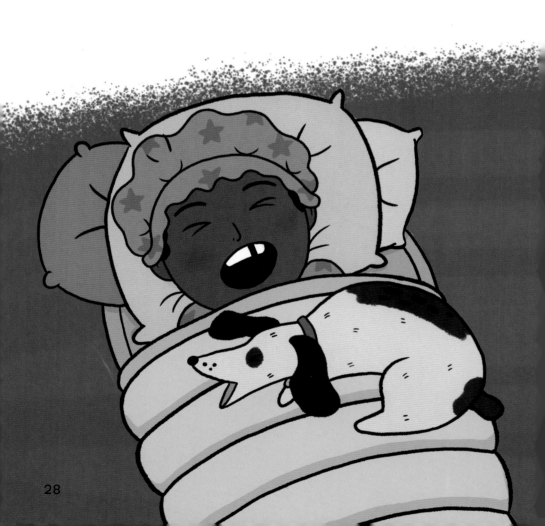

"What about the songs and s'mores
  and scary stories?" asks Mae.
"I am too sleepy," says April.
"I am wide awake,
  so I can help," says Mae.
"How?" asks April.
"I will tell a scary story
  to wake you up," says Mae.
"OK," says April.

Mae tries to think of a scary story.
It takes a long time.
At last Mae says,
"Once upon a time
there was a ghost."

"No, it was a monster,"
says Mae.

"No, it was a bear!"
says Mae.

"Hiss," says Mae's cat.
"Grrr," says April's dog.
April rolls over.

"The bear had very long arms
  and very sharp claws
  and very big teeth," says Mae.
"Hiss," says Mae's cat.

"Grrr," says April's dog softly.
April rolls over again.
"And the bear liked to
sneak up on tents," says Mae.

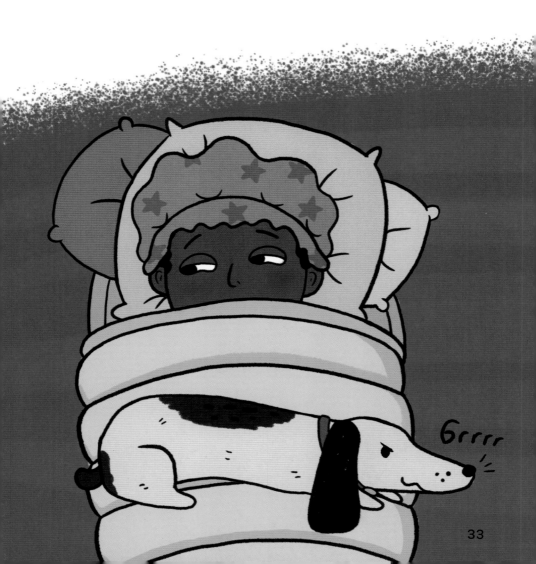

Mae thinks about the story.
What will happen next?
Then Mae hears a sound.
Is it a ghost?
Is it a monster?
Is it a bear?

No!
It is April.
It is April's dog, too.
They are snoring.

Rrrr Rrrr

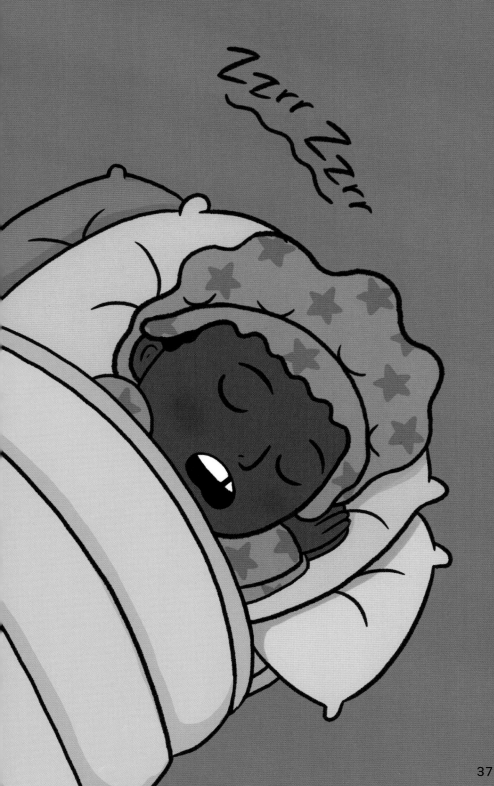

Mae laughs softly.
Mae's cat purrs softly.
Mae is still wide awake.
There will be no more
stories tonight.
There will be no s'mores
or songs.

That is OK.
April worked hard to
make them all comfy.
Mae lets April sleep.

Mae puts her head on her pillow.
Mae pulls up her sleeping bag
and her blanket.
April and her dog still snore.
Mae and her cat look at the stars.

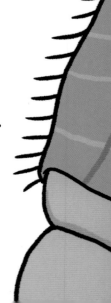

Zzrr Zzrr
Rrrr Rrrr

Another shooting star sails by.
Mae does not make a wish.
She makes a plan instead.
Even though Mae
is a night owl,
she will get up early.
She will work hard
to do something nice
for early-bird April.
She will make
s'mores pancakes for breakfast.

43

But now it is still nighttime.

It is quiet except for April's snores

and April's dog's snores.

It is dark except for the moon

and the stars.

"Good night, April," says Mae softly.

"Snore," says April.

"Snore," says April's dog.

"Purr," says Mae's cat.

"Good night, reader,"
says this book.